The Karate Kid

Based on the film
written by **ROBERT MARK KAMEN**
and directed by **JOHN G. AVILDSEN**

Illustrated by **KIM SMITH**

QUIRK BOOKS
PHILADELPHIA

Freddie B 3D

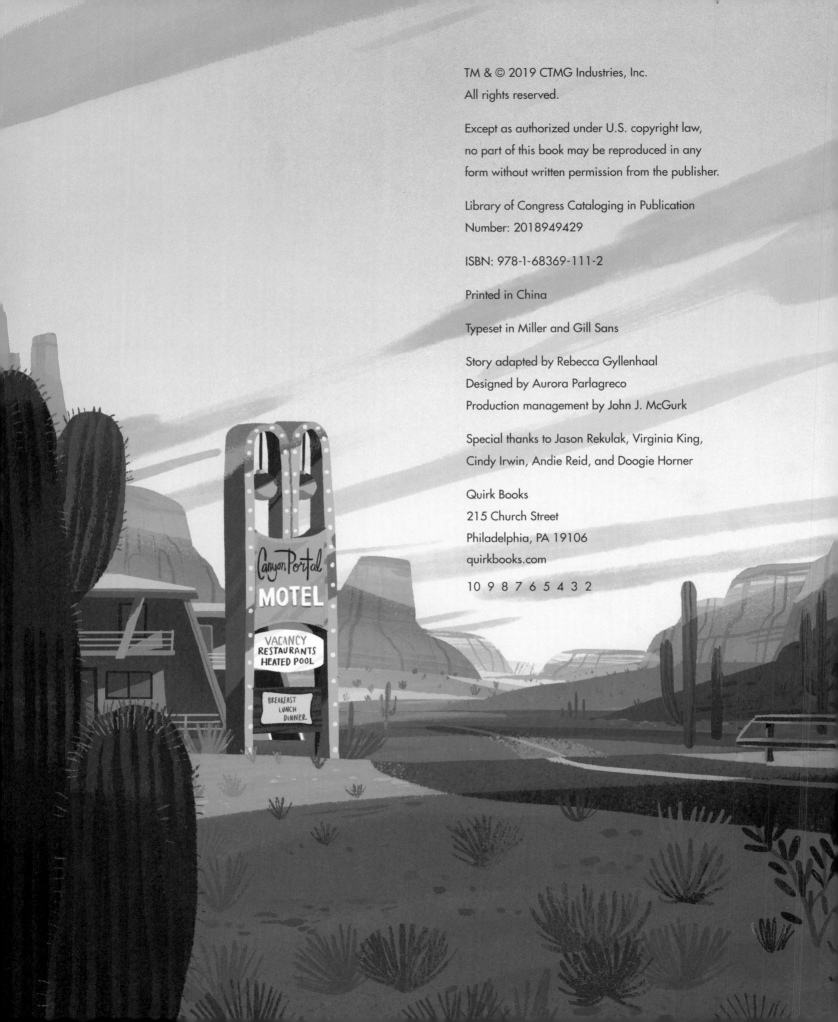

Library of Congress Cataloging in Publication
Number: 2018949429

ISBN: 978-1-68369-111-2

Printed in China

Typeset in Miller and Gill Sans

Story adapted by Rebecca Gyllenhaal
Designed by Aurora Parlagreco
Production management by John J. McGurk

Special thanks to Jason Rekulak, Virginia King,
Cindy Irwin, Andie Reid, and Doogie Horner

Quirk Books
215 Church Street
Philadelphia, PA 19106
quirkbooks.com

10 9 8 7 6 5 4 3 2

The big day had finally arrived!
Daniel and his mother had moved to California.
They were excited to live by the ocean, but Daniel
was nervous about being the new kid.

On Daniel's first day of school, some mean kids started picking on him. The leader of the group was named Johnny.

The mean kids studied karate at a dojo named Cobra Kai.

A dojo is a place where students learn martial arts.

All of the students at Cobra Kai were training
for a big karate tournament.

The next day, the Cobra Kai students chased Daniel home from school.

Suddenly, out of nowhere, a man appeared
and he chased the boys away with his karate moves.

It was Mr. Miyagi, the Japanese maintenance man who worked in Daniel's apartment building. He was better at karate than the Cobra Kai students!

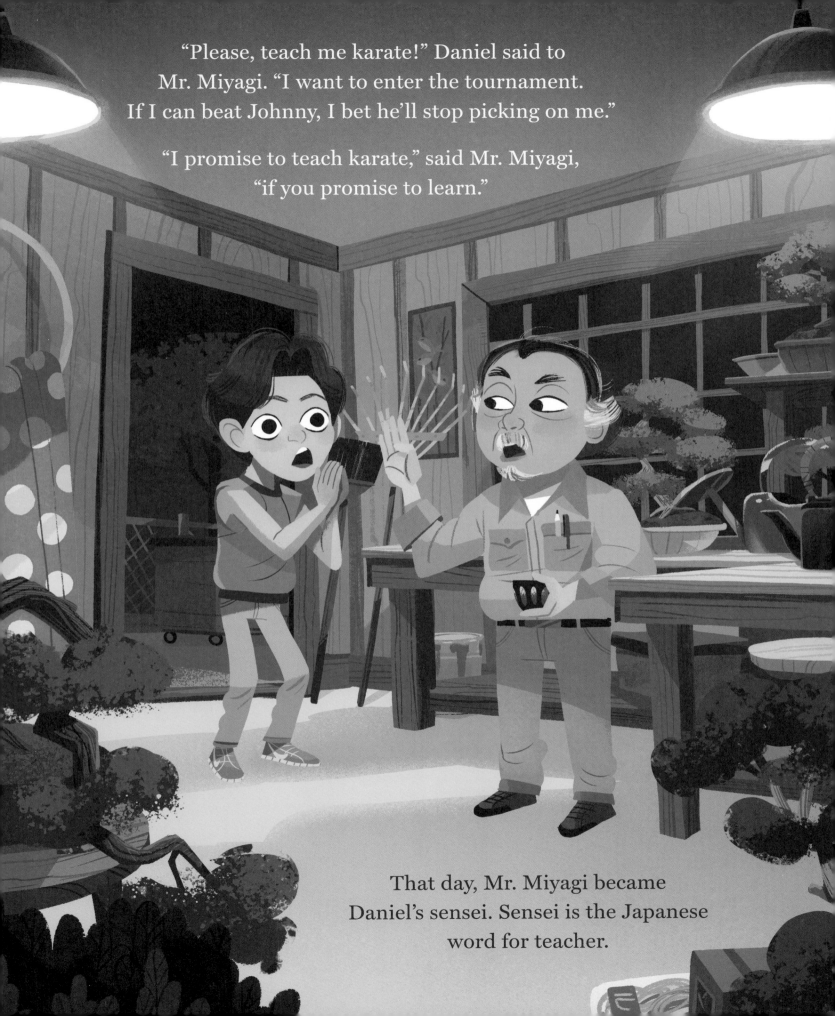

"Please, teach me karate!" Daniel said to Mr. Miyagi. "I want to enter the tournament. If I can beat Johnny, I bet he'll stop picking on me."

"I promise to teach karate," said Mr. Miyagi, "if you promise to learn."

That day, Mr. Miyagi became Daniel's sensei. Sensei is the Japanese word for teacher.

The next day, Daniel went to
Mr. Miyagi's house. Daniel was excited
to start learning karate!

First, Mr. Miyagi gave Daniel
a special headband.

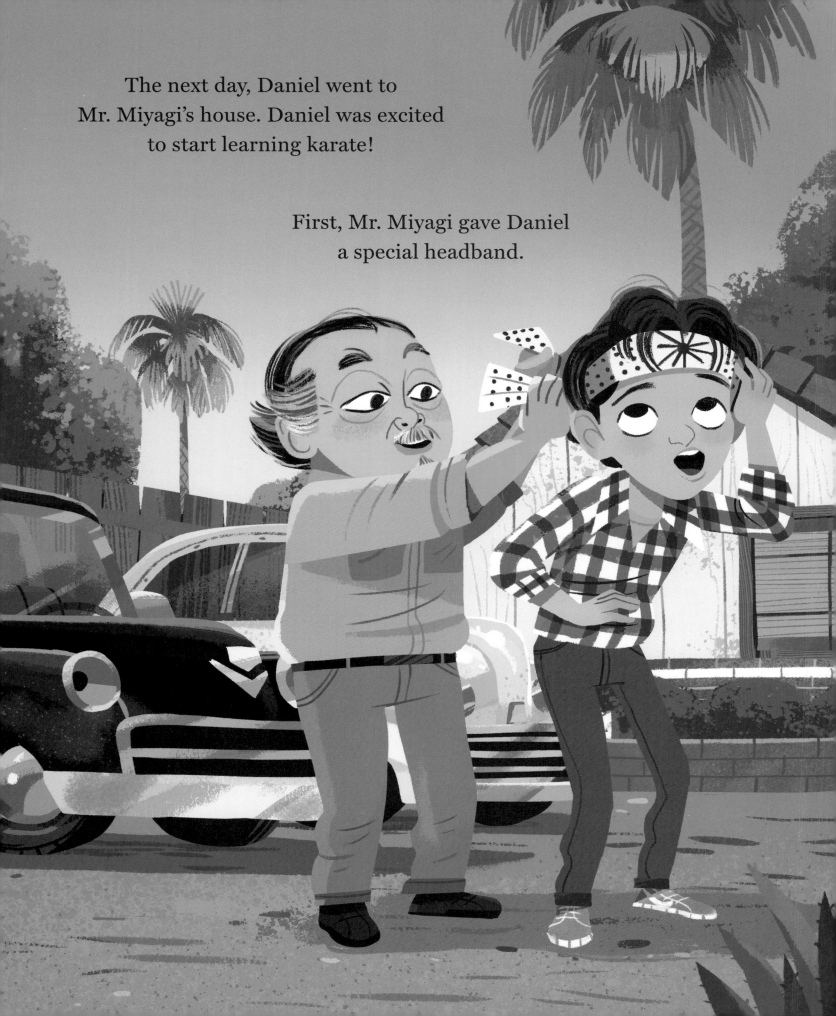

Next, Mr. Miyagi handed Daniel a bucket and a sponge. He told him to wash all the cars in the driveway, and then wax them, too!

Wax on, right hand.
Wax off, left hand.
Wax on, wax off!

Daniel worked very hard all day.

He worked until the sun went down.

Finally, all the cars were clean and shiny.

But he worked so hard and so long
that there was no time left for karate training.

Daniel worked very hard
all day.

He worked until the sun
went down.

Finally, the deck was smooth.
But he worked so hard and so long
that there was no time left for
karate training.

Daniel worked very hard
all day. He worked until the
sun went down.

Finally, the house was painted. But Daniel was frustrated.
He wanted to learn karate, not do chores all day!

When Mr. Miyagi came home, Daniel said,
"I'm tired of doing chores! Why won't you teach
me karate? I haven't learned anything!"

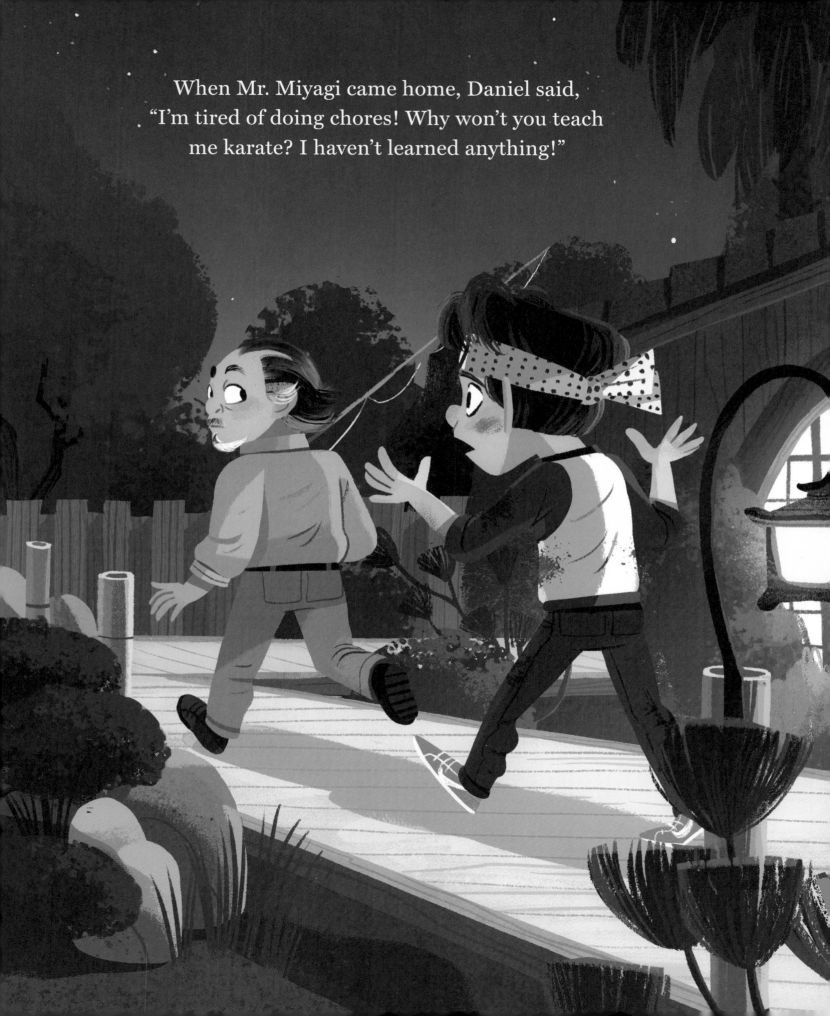

You've learned plenty. Show me how you waxed the cars.

Daniel showed him how, and he blocked Mr. Miyagi's punch.

Show me how you sanded the deck.

Daniel showed him how, and he blocked Mr. Miyagi's kick.

Daniel showed him how, and he blocked Mr. Miyagi's strike.

Daniel couldn't believe it! The whole time he thought
he was doing chores, he had actually been learning
karate moves—and getting stronger every day!

The tournament was coming up, and Daniel was practicing very hard. Mr. Miyagi taught him to balance by staying upright in the ocean waves.

Balance is key.
Balance good, karate good.
Everything good.

Mr. Miyagi taught him a special move called the crane kick,
which Daniel practiced while balancing on the edge of a boat.

He also taught Daniel that karate wasn't about fighting.
It was about balance and discipline, both in the body and in the mind.

Daniel noticed that Mr. Miyagi was always trying to catch flies with his chopsticks. One day, Daniel asked him why.

If you can catch a fly with chopsticks, you can accomplish anything.

Daniel decided to try, and he immediately caught the fly!

Beginner's luck.

Finally, it was the day of the tournament.
Daniel wore a special uniform that was a gift from Mr. Miyagi.

Daniel was very nervous.

KI-YA!

HUH!

Most of the kids were bigger than he was, and they all had black belts.

But Daniel won one match after another.

KLOK!

He just imagined he was
back at Mr. Miyagi's house,
doing his chores.

The final match was against Johnny,
the leader of the Cobra Kai students.

Daniel scored two points.

Then Johnny scored two points.

One more point would determine the winner.
Daniel stood on one leg and closed his eyes,
pretending he was in the boat on the water. Daniel found
his balance. He breathed in, and breathed out.

Daniel won the last point! He won the tournament!

Johnny handed Daniel the trophy.
"You earned it," Johnny said.

"I couldn't have done it without
my sensei," Daniel said.